William Boylston Rotch

Rambles about Amherst

William Boylston Rotch

Rambles about Amherst

ISBN/EAN: 9783337401948

Printed in Europe, USA, Canada, Australia, Japan

Cover: Foto ©Andreas Hilbeck / pixelio.de

More available books at **www.hansebooks.com**

RAMBLES ABOUT AMHERST:

EMBRACING AN

HISTORICAL AND DESCRIPTIVE SKETCH OF THE TOWN, WITH EXTRACTS
FROM THE WRITINGS OF JAMES PARTON, POINTS OF INTEREST
IN AND ABOUT AMHERST; ALSO DESCRIPTIONS OF
SOME OF THE MANY INTEREST-
ING DRIVES.

————

BY WILLIAM B. ROTCH.

————

WITH MAP OF THE HIGHWAYS.

————

AMHERST, N. H.
FARMERS' CABINET PRESS.
1890.

NOTE.

In publishing this little sketch I have not aimed at recording history, only to group together some of the interesting facts which pertain to Amherst and vicinity, that they may be more readily accessible to the stranger and those desirous of gaining a better acquaintance with the historic town. The preparation and printing of this little volume has occupied only such time as I could spare from my regular work, which will, in part, perhaps, account for its fragmentary appearance.

The greatest compensation which I expect to receive for the labor and expense involved, has been already attained, in the satisfaction of a better acquaintance with my native town and an increased love for her "dells and hills, her rocks and rills."

Hoping that those who could have done this work so much better will be kind in their criticisms, I am

Respectfully Yours,

W. B. ROTCH.

RAMBLES ABOUT AMHERST:

CHAPTER I.

HISTORICAL.

Amherst (Souhegan West) was early the home of the Narragansett tribe of Indians. The original grant from the Massachusetts General Court to the early settlers included the townships of Milford and Mont Vernon, and a portion of Merrimack. It was incorporated as a town on the 18th of January, 1760, and one of the early incorporated towns in New Hampshire. It received its name from General Jaffrey Amherst, Commander of the British forces in North America.

Early written history records the many hardships undergone by these settlers in subduing the elements, laying low the giants of the forest and making the land habitable.

In 1794, the inhabitants of that part of Amherst known as the "South West Parish," having increased to such proportions as would seem to warrant it, petitioned to the General Court to be disconnected from the township of Amherst, and incorporated as the town of Milford, which request was granted, including a tract of land from the township of Hollis.

In 1803, the "Second Parish," located upon the elevation northwesterly of Amherst, petitioned to the General Court to be set off as a separate township, which request, as in the previous instance was granted, and the town of Mont Vernon was incorporated.

For fifty years following the disconnection of these two towns Amherst was in the hey-day of its prosperity, and by far the most important place in this section of the State. It was the shire town and all of the courts were held here, and many public gatherings of much importance. The largest population Amherst ever had was before the town was divided. The census of 1790 shew a population of 2,396. In 1820 the inhabitants numbered 1,622. The village contained about 60 dwellings, a meeting - house, school house, two taverns, court house, jail, printing-office, card factory and five stores ; also two law offices.

In those "good old times" often referred to by the grey whiskered residents, Amherst did not have its present quiet, sleepy appearance of a "deserted village." The frequent sessions of the court, the annual muster and trainings, the great amount of travel to and fro over the turnpike, and its being the mailing point to all the surrounding country, served to make Amherst a business centre and busy place. But these days are past. The rapid growth of surrounding towns with available water privileges and better railroad facilities have drawn upon its vitality and greatly detracted from its business importance. The courts are no longer held here, and the county offices are now at Nashua. Aside from the general aspect of neatness every where noticeable, we have little evidence of the thrift which once abounded here.

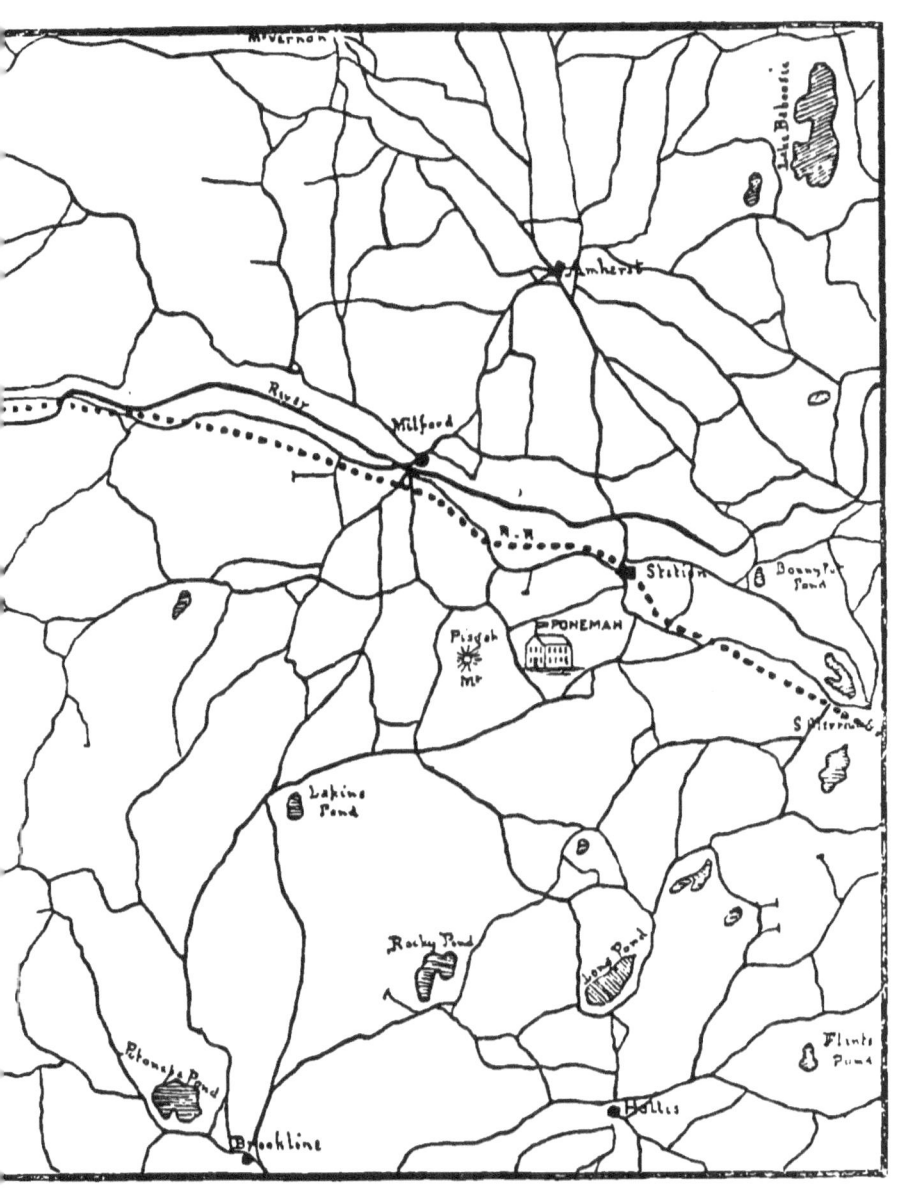

MAP OF HIGHWAYS IN AMHERST AND VICINITY.

CHAPTER II.

Amherst, in the County of Hillsborough, is 48 miles northwest of Boston, 11 miles northwest of Nashua and 12 miles southwest of Manchester. It is located on the Boston and Lowell division of the Boston and Maine Railroad, and one hour and forty-eight minutes' ride from Boston. Passengers taking the cars at the old Boston and Lowell passenger station on Causeway street, find the ride to Amherst a most delightful one and the time passes altogether too quickly. From Lowell to Nashua the train skirts along the banks of the Merrimack river, of which most delightful views can be had, and now and then glimpses of mountains and hills in the distance. Arriving at Amherst-station accommodations are found to convey passengers in either direction—to Hotel Ponemah, located one mile south, or to the village, three miles to the north. Reaching the village, stables will be found well equipped with conveniences for carrying passengers or parties to houses located at a distance or to points of interest, in and about the town. Amherst village, which is one of the most beautiful in the state, is located upon a plain of about one half mile in extent, surrounded by hills, and is thought by many to have once been the bed of a lake, whose waters found an outlet through Beaver Brook, now familiarly known as "Quoquinnapassakessananagnog," the name given by the Indians to the lands about the mouth of that brook, three miles below the village.

The village is at once noticeable for its clean, wholesome and well kept appearance ; is comprised of about 130 dwellings, each one of which shows evidence of local pride in its owner in making its outward appearance pleasant to the eye. The streets are broad with sidewalks, lined with shade trees, whose over-reaching branches and thick foliage form almost a canopy, and under whose cool shade in the hot summer days it is a delight to stroll. The soil of the "plain" is a sandy loam, of not such strength as to insure large returns from the efforts of gardening, but of sufficient firmness to support a thick mat of grass which everywhere softens the landscape and rests the eye. In the village a large tract of land has been neatly fenced in for a public common, and thickly set with maple and elm trees, which promise in the near future to make this locality a very popular resort. Rising from the centre of this common is a flag staff of very graceful proportions.

In addition, the village has three churches, handsome brick school house, ample and commodious town hall, which furnishes accommodations for the different orders and the

public library, chapel, engine house, kit factory, saw and
grist mill and one planing mill, printing office, besides
five stores and a harness-shop. There is no public house
in the village at present, fire destroying in 1876 the commodious hotel built by the citizens and which during its
brief existence was the pride of the town. The way-farer
has no trouble, however, in finding desirable accommodations
under the hospitable roofs of the several private houses
whose proprietors open their doors to unobjectionable
persons. A soldiers' monument graces a central point in the
village, and attests to the sacredness with which the citizens
hold in memory the deeds of the soldiers in the late war.
There are other points of interest in the village, not the
least among which is the old burying ground near the town
house, the old jail, long out of use, of which we shall say
more later.

From the hills which surround the village charming and
extensive views of the surrounding country can be had.
"Chestnut Hills" to the north is the highest prominence;
"Christian Hill" in the west, so named from the number of
active church members and officers it has furnished in past
days; "David's Hill" in the south, up which winds an enchanting lane, is well worthy a climb, in repay for which a
beautiful view of the village may be had, nestling down in
its quiet repose among the trees below, the church spires
only rising above their tops, and the white houses hardly
visible through the dense foliage. "Walnut Hill" in the
east is noticeable from all points for its symmetrical proportions. From either of these elevations named, high moun-

tains in the distance appear to one's gaze, which, with the
intervening valleys, furnish a panoramic scene of rare
extent, beauty and granduer.   Before continuing this sketch
and describing the character of the country adjacent
to the village, with its attractive drives and many points
of interest and note, I will give place to the graphic dis-
cription of James Parton, Horace Greeley's biographer, who,
in the interest of his friend and patron, once visited this
town and the early home of Greeley. With a little change
his words would be as applicable to-day as at the time they
were written, many years ago :—

"The village of Amherst is a pleasant place.   Seen from
the summit of a distant hill, it is a white dot in the middle
of a level plain, encircled by cultivated and gently sloping
hills.   On a near approach the traveller perceives that it is
a cluster of white houses, looking as if they had alighted
among the trees and might take wing again.   On enter-
ing it he finds himself in a very pretty village, built round
an ample green, and shaded by lofty trees.   It contains three
churches, a printing office, a court house, a jail, a half dozen
stores, an exceedingly minute watch maker's shop and a
hundred private houses.   There is not a human being to be
seen, not a sound to be heard, except the twittering of the
birds overhead, and the distant whistle of a locomotive,
which in those remote regions serves to make the silence
audible.   The utter silence and deserted aspect of the older
villages in New England are remarkable.   In the morning
and evening there is some appearance of life in Amherst ;
but in the hours of the day, when the men are at work, the

women busy with their household affairs, and the children at school, the visitor may sit at the window of the village tavern for an hour at a time and not see a living creature. Occasionally a pedler, with sleigh bells round his horse, goes

BIRTHPLACE OF HORACE GREELEY,
Founder of the N. Y. *Tribune.*

jingling by. Occasionally a farmer's wagon drives up to one of the stores. Occasionally a stage, rocking in its leather suspenders, stops at the post office for a moment, and then

rocks away again.   Occasionally a doctor passes in a very
antiquated gig.   Occasionally a cock crows, as though it
was tired of the dead silence.   A New York village, a quar-
ter the size and wealth of Amherst, makes twice its noise
and bustle.   Forty years ago, however, when Horace Greeley used to come to the stores there, it was a place of somewhat more importance and more business than it is now,
for Manchester and Nashua have absorbed many of the little streams of traffic which used to flow toward the county
town.   It is a curious evidence of the stationary character
of the place, that the village paper which had fifteen hundred
subscribers when Horace Greeley was three years old, and
learned to read from it, has fifteen hundred subscribers and
no more at this moment.   It bears the same name it did
then, is published by the same person, and adheres to the
same party."

   The township of Amherst contains about eight square
miles of better land than the average land of New England.
Wheat cannot be grown on it to advantage, but it yields
fair returns of rye, oats, potatoes, Indian corn, and young
men ; the last named of which commodities forms the chief
article of export. The farmers have to contend with hills,
rocks, stones innumerable, sand, marsh and long winters :
but a hundred years of tillage have subdued these obstacles
in part, and the people generally enjoy a safe and moderate
prosperity.   Yet, severe is their toil.   To see them plough-
ing along the sides of those steep rocky hills, the plough
creaking, the oxen groaning, the little boy driver leaping

from sod to sod, as an Alpine boy is supposed to leap from crag to crag, the ploughman wrenching the plough round the rocks, boy and man every minute or two uniting in a prolonged and agonizing yell for the panting beasts to stop, when the plough is caught by a hidden rock too large for it to overturn, and the solemn slowness with which the procession winds, creaks and groans along, gives the languid citizen, who chances to pass by, a new idea of hard work, and a new sense of the happiness of his lot. "

If Mr. Parton should revisit Amherst to-day, he would see little change in the general appearance of the place. Time has worked great changes in the people. Thirty years have wrought changes in nearly every household. They have also brought about changes in the mode of operating the farms. In place of the slow moving ox teams he would find a pair of horses drawing a sulky plow, and other improved machinery lessening the hardships of the farmer's life. Our farmers have not been slow in adopting improved methods of tilling the soil, and we believe that the pecuniary returns from their labor is more satisfactory than formerly. The raising of cereals and potatoes for the market, in large quantities, has been superseded by butter making and milk producing, and the large intervale farms are now nearly entirely given to the latter industry, a ready market being found for milk at the R. R. station, where it is daily collected and thence transported to Boston.

LAKES AND STREAMS. — Babboosie lake, so named by the Indians once dwelling upon its shores, is located about

three miles north easterly of the village : it abounds in fish.
Little Babboosic pond is connected with the lake of larger
size by a small brook.   Jo English pond is located partly
in Amherst, Mt. Vernon, and New Boston.   Damon's pond,

SOLDIER'S MONUMENT.

ERECTED IN 1871.

a small sheet of water, is located in the north east part of
the town and Stearns's pond or more familiarly known as
"Honey Pot pond" is situated in the south part of the town.
All of these ponds contain fish to greater or less extent, but

none of them, with the exception of Babboosic, have ever
been stocked with fry.

Souhegan river crosses the southerly portion of the town,
and is spanned by two carriage bridges.   Into it flows
Beaver Brook, which traverses the whole length of the town,
starting on its course in Mont Vernon.   Babboosic brook
starts from Jo English pond, runs through the northerly
part of Amherst, through Bedford, and empties into the
Souhegan river at Merrimack.   In the trout season these
brooks furnish good fishing ground.   Granite abounds,
and quarries are operated, which yield a very fine quality
of stone.   Limestone has been found in some parts of the
town, and iron ore exists in small quantities.   Some rare
minerals and crystals have been found near the Bedford
line, but are not so plenty as to attract many searchers.
White pine is the principal timber growth.   Chestnut trees
abound and when loaded with nuts, a sharp rivalry occurs between the small boy and the squirrel to see who
shall gather the most.   Oak, somewhat rare in other sec-
tions, grows abundantly here.   Game is not as plenty as
in former times, yet the skilful hunter will not lack for
sport in hunting the grey squirrel, and partridge in their
season.   Coons are also found in the swamps and on the
mountains.

A mineral spring in the east part of the town, about two
miles from the village, has some renown for its medicinal
properties.   Also a spring located near the highway from
Amherst to Mont Vernon, is noticeable for the large amount
of soda the water contains.   There are many other points

which will appeal to the visitor with equal interest as those
already named.

CONGREGATIONAL CHURCH.

Amherst is emphatically a field for artists, abounding in
those little "bits" of natural beauty, of wooded drives,
shady nooks and cool retreats, which relieve the monotony
of a less broken country.   Whoever brings a camera here

has no difficulty in finding the desired opportunity for the exercise of his art. Almost everything desired by the artist can be found. The hay-maker in the field, the boat upon the lake, the cows grazing upon the hills, winding road-ways, lights and shadows through the trees, deep glens, rustic scenes and expansive views, can all be obtained with but comparatively little effort.

Again, the intense quiet of the place and the unobtrusiveness of its inhabitants make it a spot most desirable for those seeking complete rest from business cares and anxiety; while its mail and telephone connections with the outside world help the business man to feel that he has "an eye on his business," while recruiting his bodily strength upon its pure atmosphere, and dieting upon fresh butter, milk and cream. It is a noticeable fact that those who once visit Amherst return again. Each recurring season finds among the new faces here, familiar ones, and the periodical return of some of our summer visitors is as regular as the the movements of the birds who return each spring to the nests they deserted in the fall.

The well kept road-beds, make driving a pleasure. The opportunities for boating and fishing, etc., have given the town an increasing prominence among the summer resorts of the Granite State. The well kept boarding houses have accomodations for a large number of guests, but each season finds their capacity tested to the fullest extent.

COMMON FLOWERS.—Flora has been lavish in her gifts here. From earliest Spring to latest Fall, woodland beau-

ties abound.   First after the soft mouse - tinted and pollen-
tipped pussy willows prophesy the coming of the "merrie
month of Maie," we find the delicate hued hepaticas, purple violets and white cornell.   Almost simultaneously with
these, that universal favorite of New England, the pale,
pink and white arbutus, sweet scented and shy, hiding itself under gray rock and brown leaves, creeping and nestling lovingly into beds of moss and twining evergreen,—a
"wee, modest, crimson-tippit flower."   Side-saddle or pitch-
er plant then reddens in the field, twin flowers and inno-
cence, that associate themselves with designs on the fine,
soft lawns our grandmothers wore, peep up.   Gradually
over the brown earth and bare branches a green mist appears, then, with a rush, the world about us is a maze of
bloom and the air is full of Easter incense.   Wild cherry,
dogwood, blackberry fields, peach and apple orchards dress
themselves in bridal garments of blushing pink and purest
white.   The sweet breath of the passing breeze dallies
among the branches, sending bewildering whirls of drifting
snow out into the warm June days.   It is the romance and
dream of the year—enchanting, fair and sweet.

Then follows the joy of graduates, when in great picnic
carts they go in merry groups to gather the mountain laurel, great mounds of rosy bloom, whose warm blushes re-
calls the classical legend concerning it.   Sturdy, unap-
preciated clover, red, white and yellow ; oxeyed daisies,
black-eyed-Susans, wild roses, yellow butter - cups and
plume - like ferns star the grasses and beautify field and
roadside.   Then the chestnuts drop their bunches of strung

pearls and we feel that the spring blooming is over. The trees grow darker, the foliage more dense and the shadows in the wood deepen. August brings the clematis, fairy meadow rue and swinging blue bell, the feathery golden rod, swaying pink bean, giradias and quantities of heavy clustering buck bean. September ushers in whole families of starworts. The corn, that through the summer time tilted its shining green lances at us, ripens now to yellow, and the arnicas try to cheat us into belief of returning spring by their imitation of dandelions. The air is fragrant with the winey odor of ripening grapes. October, with magic wand, turns the bunch - berries, alders and wax-work scarlet and orange. The forests are rich in red, russet, green, yellow and brown. Down in the meadow blue gentians are found. November comes and the woods are alight with the ghostly witchery of the pale hazel bloom. There is a bursting of pods and rattling of seeds on the dead leaves, and December steps in and throws his fleecy blanket over them and shows with it, for background, the delicate vases that held the seeds with their own peculiar beauty.

CHAPTER III.

New Hampshire is renowned for the sturdy character of the men it rears. The boys of the Granite Hills inhabit every State in the Union, lending their bone and muscle to the development of new territories, as well as filling positions of honor and prominence in the older States. Amherst has furnished its full quota of young men to this great regiment, and there is probably not a city in the States but what has drawn upon its life and partaken of its vitality.

Perhaps no other one of Amherst's sons ever gained such fame in the world as Horace Greeley; perhaps none other was entitled to such eminence; certainly none other ever was before the country as candidate for President. But others have gone out from Amherst whose influence has been felt throughout the length and breadth of the land. To name all those, who, though perhaps not born within our territorial lines, yet spent the years here which shaped their course through life, would be a task of too great magnitude for us at this time, yet we cannot pass over this ground without recalling a few familiar names.

There are none left who remember William Bigelow, who was the first editor of the VILLAGE MESSENGER, and afterward had charge of the Boston Latin School. Among the pupils of this distinguished teacher was Edward Everett.

For many years the name of Atherton was synonymous with Amherst. Joshua Atherton was the first of that name to settle here. He was an able lawyer and for several years the State's Attorney General. His son, the Hon. Chas. H. Atherton, was also a lawyer of much note, once a Representative in Congress, and his son Chas. G. Atherton another lawyer of prominence and U. S. Senator.

Captain Eli Brown, in early life a resident of Amherst, afterwards was in charge of the fleet of gunboats on the coast of New England.

Joseph Cushing started the publication of the FARMERS' CABINET in 1802, built the large brick building afterwards known as "Cushing's Folly." Sold CABINET in 1809 to Richard Boylston, and removed to Baltimore.

Dr. John Farmer, a historian of note, spent the early years of his life here.

Prof. James Freeman Dana was a professor of chemistry at Dartmouth College.

Dr. Samuel L. Dana, his brother was also noted as a scientist.

Gen. Joseph Low was noted far and wide as a military character. He was once Mayor of Concord.

Col. Robert Means, was treasurer of the County for years

and was a member of the Senate and Council.

David McG. Means was a very successful business man.

Isaac Spalding and Robert Read were prominent merchants here, and the former afterwards at Nashua. By his will he bequeathed a legacy of ten thousand dollars to the town, for school purposes, to be paid on the decease of his widow.

Among the early pastors of the parish church here, was Rev. Nathan Lord, D. D., L. L. D.; he resided in the house now owned and occupied by Mr. John G. Peacock, on the turnpike leading from Amherst to Mt. Vernon. He was called from his ministry to the Presidency of Dartmouth College, which position he acceptably filled for over thirty years.

The pastor to succeed Rev. Mr. Lord, was Rev. Silas Aiken. He was called from his work here to the pulpit of Park St. church, Boston, which position he held for twelve years and then removed to Vermont.

The foregoing is but a fragmentary list of the names of some of our most honored citizens, all of whom have now passed to their reward.

Those which a younger generation will more quickly associate with Amherst, perhaps, are Campbell, Dodge, Hapgood, Lawrence, Eaton, Davis, David, Abbott, Hartshorn, Melendy, Boylston, Secombe, Clark, and many others, whose names will occur as readily to the reader as to the writer. But enough have here been recalled to make the sons of Amherst feel proud of their ancestry.

CHAPTER IV

Lake Babboosic. This beautiful sheet of water is situated two and one-half miles easterly of the village of Amherst. Is accessible from all directions by carriage roads. The Pond covers an area of about three hundred and eighty acres, and the water varies in depth to about thirty feet. Its greatest length is two miles and its greatest breadth one mile. It has long been a favorite resort for boating and fishing, and is much visited by pleasure parties and its worthy fame is every year extending. About ten years ago it was stocked with black bass by the State Board of Fish Commissioners, and fine specimens are now captured every season. The waters being fresh and not a sluggish pond, the bass are full of game, varying in size from one to five and six pounds. Other fish such as perch, abound. Boats for fishing or rowing can be had at different points along the shore. At the east side of the lake is a fine grove of pines, underneath whose shade, seats, swings, a band stand and platform for dancing have been built by Mr. Colston, the present proprietor of the Babboosie House, which is located a short walk back from the shore, upon a prominence overlooking the lake. New Hampshire has many jewels in her crown of natural beauty, but few are brighter, fairer or more beautiful, than Lake Babboosie.

Present Town House, (FORMER COURT HOUSE.)
This building was originally erected for the use of the

county Courts, which at the time were all here. Many exciting scenes have transpired within its historic walls, and many distinguished jurists have here made pleas which have helped them on the road to fame and fortune. It was not in this building, as is quite generally, but erroneously reported, that Daniel Webster, made his maiden argument, before Judge Farrar, but in the former court house, which stood just in front of the site of the dwelling of the late David Russell. This second court house, where the giants of the legal profession, including Webster, were wont to assemble, is still standing, near the old foundry building, occupied as a double tenement dwelling house. When the county offices and courts were removed from Amherst the building reverted to the town, since which time repairs and enlargements have been made, until now it is one of the most convenient and best appointed town houses in the county. The stage was lately enlarged, and a nice set of scenery donated to the town by Oscar Shaffer. It has a commodious upper and lower hall, a fire proof vault, lobby, and is the repository of the town library.

The Old Jail, as it is familiarly and rightly called, having been long out of use, is a place of some interest to those visiting Amherst village. The first jail built here was the west end of the frame building connected with the stone structure now standing, and built of heavy oak logs, erected about 1770, and the first stone building about 1810. It formerly had a high brick wall around it. Some noted criminals have been confined in this old building. From one of its cells. Farmer the murderer, rode to the scaffold, erected near the residence of the late B. B. David.

Soldiers' Monument.   The monument which graces a central spot in our village, was completed in 1871.   The granite base was cut from a bowlder, found on the farm of

RESIDENCE OF THE LATE GEORGE KENT.

Levi J. Secombe, Esq.   A figure of a soldier, in bronze, holding a musket. stands upon the granite pedestal, in

which is inserted a tablet, bearing the names of thoses en-
listing from Amherst in the late war, who lost their lives
defending the old flag.   The cost of this memorial was
$ 4000. A gift for this purpose by the late Aaron Lawrence,
was supplemented by an appropriation from the town.

RESIDENCE OF THE LATE HON. H. EATON.

The Brick Block, familiarly known as the "old
brick" was erected about 1809, by Mr. Joseph Cushing, at

that time publisher of the FARMERS' CABINET, who purpos-
ed to enter extensively into the printing and publishing
of books, and with this end in view he erected this building,
long afterwards known as "Cushing's Folly." He never
occupied it, for before its completion he hastily removed to
Baltimore. It has had numerous owners and more numerous occupants. The lower story has usually been occupied
as stores, though originally the west side as a tenement.
The upper ones have been used for school-rooms, tenements,
book bindery, pattern - makers shop, and at one time the
entire building as an iron foundry. It is owned by the
heirs of the late Hon. Harrison Eaton, and at present occupied as a store, in which is the post-office : a millinery
store and a barber shop. It is one of the land marks of
Amherst. Long may it be spared from tempest or fire, a
link between the present and the past.

Greeley's Birthplace.

The spot where Horace
Greeley first saw the light of day, is about five miles north-
easterly from Amherst village, on the first highway leading
to Bedford. The house stands as it was originally built,
and is owned and occupied as a farm house by Joseph F.
Hanson. James Parton, in writing of this spot twenty
years ago said :

"The farm owned by Zaccheus Greeley when his son
Horace was born, was four or five miles from the village of
Amherst. It consisted of eighty acres of land —heavy
land to till—rocky, moist, and uneven, worth then eight

hundred dollars, now two thousand. The house, a small, unpainted, but substantial and well-built farm-house, stood and still stands, upon a ledge or platform, half way up a high, steep, and rocky hill, commanding an extensive and almost panoramic view of the surrounding country. In whatever direction the boy may have looked, he saw rock. Rock is the feature of the landscape. There is rock in the old orchards behind the old house ; rocks peep out from the grass in the pastures : rock along the road : rock on the sides of the hills: rock on their summits: rock in the valleys : rock in the woods : rock, rock, everywhere rock. And yet the country has not a barren look. I should call it a serious looking country : one that would be congenial to grim covenanters and exiled round-heads. The prevailing colors are dark, even in the brightest months of the year. The pine woods, the rock, the shade of the hill, the color of the soil, are all dark and serious. It is a still unfrequented region. One may ride along the road upon which the house stands, for many a mile, without passing a single vehicle. The turtles hobble across the road fearless of the crushing wheel. If any one wished to know the full meaning of the word country, as distinguished from the word town, he need do no more than ascend the hill on which Horace Greeley saw the light, and look around. Such was the character of the region in which Horace Greeley passed the greater part of the first seven years of his life."

Amherst Common. The large tract of land, which is neatly fenced in, and thickly set with shade trees, will,

in the near future, be a place of much beauty.   The increased care given to the trees and soil recently, show
results in increased verdure and foliage.   In the fall, the
maples take on the hues of the rainbow, and make it a
spot of rare brilliancy.

Bank Building.   RESIDENCE OF CHAS. RICHARDSON.
This building was erected by the Hillsborough Bank and
during its short life was used as its banking house, and

residence of its cashier.   It was also used as a banking house by the Farmers' Bank from 1825 to 1843.   The vault or safe remains at present, as originally built.   The brick for this fine dwelling was made upon the Lord place, then newly built by Capt. Eli Brown.

Mineral Spring.   Located one and one half miles east of the village in a beautiful pine grove, near what was once a trotting park, is a spring widely noted for its medicinal properties.   The water is sought for by those affected by scrofulous diseases, and is used as a wash as well as taken internally, with beneficial results.   It is so heavy with iron as to discolor the banks of the brook into which it flows, for a long distance, giving them a redish shade, like iron rust.   The water is not objectionable to the taste.

In the geological survey of the State made several years ago, this spring was the only mineral spring to which attention was especially called as possessing any very remarkable medicinal properties.   Dr. Jackson and several other distinguished chemists have also since analyzed its waters, all with the same general results and tending to confirm well known facts in relation to its value.   A very careful and exhaustive analysis has been made by Prof. Babcock, and from it will be seen, that the water of this spring exhibits a combination of rare curative agents seldom found in a spring in such rich proportions.

ANALYSIS AND RESULT.

The water contains in an Imperial gallon 15.52 grains of

mineral and organic matter. This consists of the following:—

Carbonate of Lime	5.66 grains.
Carbonate of Iron	1.30 "
Carbonate of Magnesium . .	1.47 "
Carbonate of Sodium . . .	28 "
Crenic Acid	3.87 "
Sulphate of Lime	1.63 "
Sulphate of Potassium . . .	.35 "
Chloride of Sodium	.87 "
Selicia and Alumnia . . .	.09 "
Total	51.52 "

Free Carbonate Acid undetermined.

JAMES F. BABCOCK.
Analytical and Consulting Chemist.

Picnic Ground. On the land owned by the town in connection with the farm at Amherst Station, is a beautiful grove of pines. This grove has been cleared of all underbrush, seats, platform, cook houses and other conveniences arranged for picnicing parties. It is especially well adapted for large gatherings, the grounds sloping toward the centre, forming a natural amphitheatre. Its proximity to the railroad station enhances its other conveniences.

Congregational Church. This is the most prominent edifice that appears to the eye as one passes through the village. The building was originally owned by the town, and was purchased by the Congregational Society in 1832 when it was thoroughly repaired and alterations made. The town still owns the bell and steeple, and have rights in the lower story. It was for many years the only place for public meetings in town.

The first pastor was Rev. Daniel Wilkins, installed in 1741. He died in 1783. The second pastor was Rev. Jeremiah Barnard, he died in 1835. The third pastor, Rev. Nathan Lord, D. D., was settled as colleague with Mr. Barnard, May 23, 1816. He was called to the Presidency of Dartmouth College in 1828. The fourth pastor Rev. Silas Aiken, D. D. was settled March 4, 1829. He was called to the pastorial care of Park St. church, Boston, in 1837. The fifth pastor Rev. Frederick A. Adams, Ph. D., was settled Nov. 15, 1837, and dismissed Sept. 24, 1840. The sixth pastor was Rev. Wm. T. Savage, D. D., settled Feb. 24, 1840, and dismissed April, 4, 1843. The seventh pastor Rev. Josiah Gardner Davis, D. D., was settled May 22, 1844, and dismissed Jan. 22, 1880. The eighth pastor Rev. Willis D. Leland, was settled June 22, 1880, and dismissed May 16, 1883. The present pastor, Rev. Alfred J. McGown, was settled Dec. 1, 1885.

Baptist Church. This house was built about the beginning of the century by the Unitarians, and passed into the hands of the Baptist Society in 1844. The interior was recently remodelled and modernized and is now quite attractive. This church has had no less than seventeen pastors within the half century of its existence, and is at present without a permanent supply.

The Methodist Chapel was dedicated about 1828. Since then until the present the church has been closed about one half of the time. It has had several pastors of ability, and is at present supplied by Rev. Wm. Merrill of Milford.

Purgatory Falls, OR HUTCHINSON'S GROVE, in Mt. Vernon, is a place of some note and interest, and is visited yearly by thousands. It is about two miles south-west of the village. It is a deep ravene, through which flows a small stream. The chief attractions are, the canal and its outlet, the "Devil's Bean Pot," in the ledge, and the imprint of a human foot imbedded in the rock, the wash boiler and tub, a stocking, cups and saucers, etc. It is a fine sight when the canal is nearly filled with water, to see it rushing and foaming to the gulf, and then falling forty feet to the rocks below. The grove contains a double bowling ally, band stand and dancing floor. The annual basket picnic here has become an institution.

Prospect Hill, in Mont Vernon, is a point much visited by guests at the summer boarding houses, and by many others, every season. A carriage road to the summit makes the highest point easily accessible. It is best described by Prof. Bancroft, of Phillips Academy :

"To the south is seen Mt. Wachusett in Princeton, Mass.; Watatic in Ashby and Ashburnham; Barrett, Kidder and Flat Mts. in New Ipswich; the Temple, Peterboro' and Lyndeboro' ranges throughout their whole extent, of which Piscataquog lies almost exactly south-west; Crotchet Mt. rises beyond the village of Francestown, with the symmetrical cone of Lovell's

Mt. still further to the north. Kearsarge is seen on the distant horizon towards the north, flanked right and left by the Black Mts., Mission Ridge, the Mink Hills and Stewart Peak. A little east of north, only a few miles distant, the rounded summit of Joe English beetles towards the south. Turning to the right, Roby Hill, the lesser Uncanoonuc and the greater Uncanoonuc are seen, and, far beyond, the chimneys and spires of Manchester, Mt. Pawtuckawa, Saddle Back, and McCoy's in Nottingham and Allenstown. The view to the east and south-east is of a wide expanse of rolling country, dotted with villages and farms, with church spires and the buildings of the great manufactories of Nashua and Lowell. At your feet nestles the village of Amherst, and the turret of Hotel Ponemah appears above the forest beyond. In the Autumn mornings, the lines of fog mark the valleys of the Merrimack, the Nashua and the Souhegan. Thus in three quadrants of the horizon are noble mountains, near and far, solitary peaks and massive ranges, while the fourth quadrant presents a plain, stretching as far as the eye can reach, diversified by dwellings, farms, forests and streams.

Hotel Ponemah. This house is the leading summer resort in this vicinity. It is located at the celebrated Milford Springs, about one and one half miles from Milford village, and reached from Amherst Station, by coaches from the hotel, running to meet each train, in a pleasant drive of about one mile. The health giving properties of its waters are widely known, and the hotel, with its large rooms and cheerful fire places, and broad piazzas extending entirely around the house, is fast becoming equally famous. From the tower which surmounts the house an extensive view of the surrounding country is obtained, and by ascending "Mount Pisgah," near the house, a still greater expanse of country is seen. A correspondent of the Boston Post writes as follows of Hotel Ponemah and its surroundings:—

"The charms of this most delightfully situated hotel are already well known, its first three seasons being under the excellent care of Mr. Gleason of the Victoria, and conducted last summer very successfully and with well filled house by Mr. D. S. Plummer, its present proprietor. The great height of land, the superb width of view, the variety of mineral springs directly on the place, and the number of interesting drives make it a most desirable summer resort. Beautiful woods lie behind the house, where mountain laurel blooms abundantly in June, and the pure, delicious air cannot fail to improve health and strength. The spacious rooms, wide piazzas and open fire-places are attractive features, and when the access of simply two hours from Boston is mentioned there seems little to be added. A list of mountains to be seen from Hotel Ponemah was recently handed me, from which I quote verbatim: "To the north are seen Mt. Vernon, Joe English in New Boston, the Goffstown mountain, Crotchet mountain in Francestown, and on a clear day Mooselauk, Kearsarge, Sunapee and other mountains farther north. On the east may be seen the Blue Hills, running through Rochester, Barrington and Nottingham, including Chocorua, Ossipee, Saddleback, Teneriffe, Pawtuckaway, and others, also Agamenticus on the borders of Maine. From the elevated lands to the west of the house, the Lyndeborough, Temple and Greenfield mountains are visible, with lofty Monadnock and the range extending through central Massachusetts."

The following interesting account of the discovery of Milford Mineral Springs, we take from the FARMERS' CABINET, of the date of December 5th, 1818. The story is corroborated by several similar accounts published in other papers of about that date:—

Mr. Boylston :

My son, Willie Sargent, was taken sick in February last of a consumption, and continued in a gradual decline till the 19th of August, when he died. On Monday the 13th of July, he fell asleep in the forenoon, and had a dream or vision, in which he saw a man standing by a rock in a piece of woodland near my house, who told him there was a spring where he stood, under ground, the water of which by drinking, would cure a consumption. On the next night he again dreamed of seeing the man in the same place, who told him as before of the spring. And again on the night of the 8th of August he the third time had the same vision, and the man repeated the assurance of there being a spring where he stood; and of its being a cure for the consumption. He also said his name was Gabriel. He did not tell my son the water would cure him in particular, nor did Willie expect it would, but said it would help others, and was very anxious to have it found. Some persons dug at some distance from the rock, and found a spring of water of clayey appearance, which would not settle clear, etc., and which has been represented as the spring described by *the man*; but my son said it could not be in the right place, nor was the water such as he expected to find it. He wished to be carried to the ground that he might point out the spot where he was told the spring lay. Accordingly, on the Monday following his last dream, we carried him on to the ground, it being about 70 rods from my house, and he readily showed us the rock by which the man stood, he being well acquaintee with the place. He directed us to dig by the side of the rock, which was done to the depth of 7 feet; but from the appearance of the ground and the extreme dryness of the season there was not the least indication of water, and we gave up the undertaking. But he was not satisfied and continued anxious about it, till the hour of his death, being fully persuaded such a spring would be found. After his death I procured a person acquainted in using the mineral rod, who, on trying his instruments, decided on the very spot where we had before dug, as directed by my son, and foretold by the man in his dream. After digging about three feet deeper than before, we indeed came to a spring, which flowed freely, and on being stoned up contains water several feet deep. This water is perfectly clear. It has been drank by a great many people. On some it has operated as an emetic, on others differently, and on others again it has no sensible effect. A number of invalids have resorted to it, and in some cases they have thought they found relief.

EBENEZER SARGENT.

Bedford Ravine, (OR DEVIL'S PULPIT.) This most

wonderful natural curiosity, which attracts many visitors each summer, is situated in Bedford, and can be reached from Amherst by a drive of about 5 miles, which takes one by the Greeley house, or, by a more circuitous route, by way of "Chestnut Hills." It is only within a few years that this strange freak of nature has been accessible without a fatiguing walk of a mile or more. But since the road-way was completed by Mr. French, upon whose land this wonderful chasm is situated, this place has gained a much wider renown. It is doubtless unparelled in this section of New England. A pen picture would utterly fail to describe the wildness of this spot. It has the appearance of an

"unfinished corner" of the world. The time to visit
it is in the Spring, or after a great storm, when the
brook that courses through it is filled with water, and goes
dashing and foaming over the rocks and falling a great

RESIDENCE OF THE LATE B. B. DAVID.

distance to the gulf below. The "freaks" which have been
named, and the imaginative visitor can discover many more
to which he can apply the name that most readily suggests

itself, and probably with equal appropriateness, are these: The "churn," "bed-room, with chamber above," "elephant's head," "Indian stairway," "bottomless pit," "fallen rocks," "arch," "oven," "boiling pot," "devil's foot prints," and the "well." This is a very interesting place and no one visiting in its vicinity should return without seeing it.

Barnes' Falls. This fall is situated in a secluded spot about two miles above Wilton, nine miles from Amherst. It is reached by a rough pathway branching from the main road, leading over little steep hills until one suddenly finds himself on the plateau of the greater hill of which these form the stairs. Teams are left here and the field to the left traversed and the roar of the trembling water comes to the ear. Here we find the fall, a stream which has a descent of about fifty feet, width of perhaps twenty between its banks, upon which ferns cluster and shrubs bend and dip. It is wild, beautiful and comparatively little known.

The First Jail. That King George the Third had a jail in Amherst is satisfactorily established, and that it was within the present dwelling of William Rhodes, one-half mile below the village, then the residence of Col. Robert Reed. (See Hilsborough County Congress p. 46.) That it was not very secure is equally evident, as the Court of General Sessions, October, 1772, authorized the Sheriff to employ a guard of four men to prevent escape of prisoners. In 1773 the place was purchased by Joshua Atherton, Esq.

which may account for the fact that he, and other political prisoners from this county, were incarcerated at Exeter until the completion of the new jail.

RESIDENCE OF REV. DR. DAVIS.

This place is of more than passing interest, not only because of its present appearance, located as it is underneath the shadowing branches of several majestic elms, together with the fact of its being for so many years the residence of Dr. Matthias Spalding, but to this is added the interesting circumstance that within its walls were held the first meetings of Benevolent Lodge F. and A. M. organized here in 1797, and removed to Milford in 1826. Samuel Dana was the first Worshipful Master of this lodge.

Organizations. SOUTHEGAN GRANGE, No. 10 Patrons

of Husbandry. Organized here December 5, 1873, with sixteen charter members, and is now one of the largest and most flourishing Granges in the State. It holds its regular meetings for Grange work, the discussion of topics of interest to farmers, and literary exercises, on the Thursday on or preceeding the full of the moon, and the second Thursday following.

CHAS. H. PHELPS POST, G. A. R. Was instituted here July 10th, 1879. Joseph B. Fay was its first Commander. Meetings are held monthly, on Saturday evening.

UNITED ORDER of the GOLDEN CROSS. Instituted July 1, 1881, with twenty-seven charter members. A co-operative life insurance order, paying a weekly sick benefit and pledging mutual protection in health and sickness to its members. Officers elected semi-annually. Members now number seventy-five. Meets semi-monthly, on Wednesday evenings.

ANCHOR LODGE, ORDER of ÆGIS. Instituted Aug. 26, 1889 with twenty-two charter members, by Chas. H. Robinson, of Lynn, Mass. A co-operative insurance order. Meets semi-monthly, on Tuesday evening.

CHAS. H. PHELPS WOMAN'S RELIEF CORPS, was organized soon after the Post. For a time the charter was given up. It was re-organized Dec. 3, 1889, and is now in a flourishing condition with a large membership. Its meetings are held semi-monthly, on Saturday evening.

Town Library. MRS. E. M. BURNHAM, Librarian.

Whatever Amherst may lack in social and educational advantages is in a measure compensated by a well selected, and liberally patronized library. Under the careful and judicious supervision of Rev. Dr. Davis, who has served for ten years as chairman of the Board of Trustees, the library as a public institution has yearly grown in popular favor and patronage. It now comprises two thousand volumes, embracing works of history, poetry, biography, fiction, and some valuable books of reference. The library is located in the town house, in a room used in conjunction with the Selectmen for their business meetings. The present quarters are poorly adapted for its use, and it is sincerely hoped that in the near future some plan may be devised, either by the town, or suggested by some philanthropic disposed person, by which the library can have separate apartments, or, better still, a building entirely devoted to its use. The library rooms are open to the public twice each week, on Saturday afternoon and Thursday evening.

The following extract, showing the inception and growth of this institution, is taken from a late report of the library Trustees :

"March 9, 1859, at a little gathering at the residence of William Wetherbee, Esq., it was proposed that there be a society formed for the purpose of meeting together from time to time and purchasing books to be circulated among the members of the society."

Such is the modest record of the movement out of which grew the organization of the Amherst Library Association. Among the most active of the early members of this Society, we find the names of Mrs. P. W. Jones and sister Mrs. M. M. Peaslee, Dea. B. B. David, David Stewart, Lucy W. Blunt, J. B. Fay, C. B. Tuttle, Cathraine Boylston, Elizabeth Wilkins, Dr. F. P. Fitch, Jonathan Knight, all of whom have deceased, Messrs. Hapgood and Abbott, E. S. Cutter, Esq., Wm. A. Mack, John F. Whiting, Mary D. Moore, now Mrs. French, who have removed from town and a few others who are still living to witness the fruits of this praiseworthy undertaking.

The plan ripened into fruitfulness by the adoption of a constitution, and by-laws, for "the establishing of a miscellaneous Library of useful books." The initiation fee was twenty-five cents at first, with a monthly payment of ten cents. The payment for membership was subsequently advanced to fifty cents, and some literary entertainments were provided by which to enlarge the funds of the Association. The money so raised was expended in the purchase of

books and the collecton was placed in charge of some me-
chanic or shopkeeper in the village whose place of business
was easy of access.   We notice the names of Stevens.
Russell, Merrill, Few and Walker as librarians, the office
involved continued care and the compensation was small.
The position was not coveted and the Library had a peri-
patetic life.   The organization was fluctuating in its mem-
berhip by reason of the inevitable changes in the commun-
ity and at times the Society was near dissolution.   But the
Library had already demonstrated its beneficent uses and
and its friends were roused to prevent its waste or disper-
sion.

In 1870 a special effort was made to revive the Association: a large addition was made to the membership : the constitution was revised : the membership fee was raised to one
dollar and regular meetings successfully instituted.   A
catalogue was prepared and printed containing 427 titles.
The year following the Selectmen granted the use of the
petit jury room as a depository for the Library and the
Executive Committee employed Mrs. E. M. Burnham as
Librarian. The room was opened every Saturday P. M. for
the accommodation of its patrons. New books were purchased, an additional book case, presented by Miss Sarah Lawrence, made the collection more attractive. The circulation
was very much enlarged: many volumes were loaned to
persons not enrolled with the organization.   Generous con-
tributions in books were made by Mrs. Conant, Miss L. F.
Boylston and other friends of the Institution.

In 1873, provision was made for incorporating the Association under the General Statutes. To meet the increasing expenses the members submitted to successive annual assessments. Meanwhile the Library was becoming more widely known, and its advantages as an auxilliary to the system of public instruction were generally recognized. A sentiment gradually gained currency that the books should be accessible to all classes of our citizens and that the town might rightfully bear the expense of maintaining the Institution. Accordingly in Febuary 1879, the Association appointed a committee "to see if the town of Amherst will accept and maintain the Library now held by this Association and fix on the conditions on which this arrangement shall be carried into effect."

An article was inserted in the warrant for the Town Meeting, viz:—"To see if the town will vote to accept the Library now held by the Amherst Library Association, and establish and maintain the same by suitable appropriations as a Public Library for the use of the citizens of Amherst, aggreeably to the provisions of Chapthr 46 of the General Statutes of New Hampshire.

The motion to accept the Library prevailed and the Selectmen in conjunction with the Superintending School Committee, were instructed to make all necessary rules for the use and maintenance of the Library The next year, 1880, the appropriation was increased and the Library was placed in charge of a Board of Trustees, an arrangement which continues in force to this day. In the ten years now clos-

ing, the number of books has increased from 680 volumes
to 1755 volumes, 4 books being discarded. Of this large
addition 719 volumes have been acquired by purchase and
371 volumes, more than one third of the enlargement,
have been the gift of friends.

In placing this sketch of the origin and progress of the
Library in their Annual Report, the trustees are animated
by a desire to keep alive the memory of those who projected this scheme, and to recognize gratefully the persistent
zeal with which their successors have cherished and per-
fected the enterprise. The usefulness of the Library is ac-
knowledged by all, and the frequent generous donations of
books, by which its shelves have been enriched, illustrate
the esteem in which it is held by those who love the town."

CHAPTER V.

SOME INTERESTING DRIVES.

AMHERST MINERAL SPRING AND AROUND THE POND.

The drives about Amherst are many and beautiful, each with its own peculiar feature, which renders it delightful.

The first, which the stranger is usually taken, though not the most beautiful, is perhaps as full of interest as any, is to the Spring and around the Pond. This road to the Spring is level and shaded, lying through woods until the spot is nearly reached. This Spring lies in a meadow, behind a small grove of large pines, and is approached by a path crossing a field, in which runs the nearly effaced

track of the old race course. This Spring is rich in iron
solution, and is recomended quite extensively by local phy
sicians, for irritations of all sorts, except temper. From
this point the drive to the pond is not so pretty, though a
pleasant glimpse of the mountains is obtained. The Lake
itself is a pretty sheet of water about two miles long and
one wide. As we sit in a boat in the middle of the Pond
and watch the water gleaming and dimpling in the cool
breeze and note the long reflections of the purpling hills,
and the glowing sky, we wonder if Elliot gathered his dusky
audience about him on these shores We wonder as we
listen to the mocking echo fling back the bugle call into
the bugler's lips, if in those times Dame Echo sent
back a less musical note, responding to the fierce war cries
and savage yells, or if it gave a tender reply to the song
of some swarthy lover.

From the Pond, directly to the village, the drive is short,
and of no especial interest, except in the memory of those
who, on some summer's day have replenished their rose jars
with the spicy odor of old fashioned damask roses—the way-
side legacy bequeathed the passer-by, from some old time
garden.

Another route, leading us around the Pond, is both beautiful and full of interest. The first point, Grater hill, we
take pleasure in for two reasons, its lovely view of the lake
and mountains beyond, and because here is the reputed home
for a time, of one of the most gifted women of modern time,
Margaret Fuller Ossoli. It is an old fashioned house, with

a monstrous chimney. One of those wide mouthed chimneys that tells of the cheery crackling of the open fire, before which merry youngsters and happy oldsters sat and crack nuts and roast apples and tell stories. Why, one can almost smell the odor of the juicy fruit as it sputters and sizzles and browns before the heat. The house is fast falling to decay and before very long another old landmark will have disappeared.

Skirting along the shore of the lake the road winds pleasantly, the sparkling water glancing, now here, now there, through the heavy umbrage of the trees. We pass a little low house, set far in from the road. Here Dr. Payson, an eminent divine and the father of Mrs Prentiss is said to have lived for a short time—a man so beloved and saintly, as to make it almost hallowed ground. We also pass the old Merrimack poor farm, now used as a private dwelling. In this vicinity there are two or three good boarding houses which are filled during the summer months with a good class of patronage. We come now out on the Manchester road, following which we arrive shortly at the village.

OVER DUNCKLEE HILL.

We use always the village as our centre, and the roads leading away from it as the radii reaching to our desired points of interest. This time the spoke of our wheel chosen, is that highway leading directly to Amherst Station. Arriving at this point, and going a little further, we come to a fork

in the road. We choose the one leading to the right and keep
to the right.   At the next division we find a tiny bridge
and laugh at the ambitious performance of a miniature Ni-
agra and find ourselves at the foot of the hill.   It is a hard
climb of about a half mile in length.   When nearly at the
top there is another disagreement in the highway.   The
road parts company with itself, one side leading to the
large summer hotel —Hotel Ponemah, and the Milford
Springs.   The turn of the other leading to the summit
of Duncklee Hill.   In the various seasons this hill abounds
with the most beautiful specimens of arbutus, laurel, golden
rod and clematis.   Arbutus and laurel especially are of
finer quality and more abundant here than in any other
place we can recall.

As we come out upon the open hill top, far ahead of us
and around us are the hills and the mountains.   The dark
pine forest deepening the valley, seems to place the mountains farther away.   Away up here where the air blows
fresh and sweet, the sight of the encircling mountains, the
clear sunshine and peace make the mind involuntarily turn
to that other hill country we have been told about in far off
Judea, and we think of that encircling Love, and the
strength of it.   Oh, those hills, with the dappling shadows
of the clouds lifting—shifting—drifting—over them!   The
world is beautiful—God made it so, and pronounced it
"good"—why not go out into the hills and country sides
and look upon it and let it grow into us more?

The whole extent of Temple, Peterborough and Lynde-

boro' ranges lie directly before us : to the left, Mt. Wachusett, in Princeton Mass. Wattatic, in Ashby, and many
others. Down at our feet is busy Milford. Over beyond
the village we can trace the outline of the Souhegan, but
we get no gleam of the water. Descending the hill, we
come directly into the heart of the lively little town. Here
we find all trades and many of the professions fairly well
represented.

We pass through the village leaving the common to
our left, and cross the stone bridge keeping to the right.
About a half mile out of Milford, we come to a point where
we may make a choice of ways back to Amherst. One
the direct route and the new highway, the other more en-
ticing and somewhat longer, leading through a shady by-
way, once the travelled road between Milford and Amherst.
To follow this last, we turn to the right, and, after crossing
one road, keep watch along the left for a break in the wall
where a path, slightly worn is seen. Turning in here we
find ourselves in some one's broad ten acre lot. Here in
June the ground blackberry is so closely mattted and thickly blossomed, it looks as if a scurrying flight of snowflakes
had fallen there, a little later, and we find thick patches of
luscious wild strawberries. Later, the grasses grown tall,
sway in the breezes, their gleaming stems making silvery
billows of light across to the shade of the sweet apple tree
by the wall : wild flowers bloom in the track of the old ditch
and here and there black-eyed-Susans and meadow ferns
mingle with the grasses. Golden-rod—tiny golden elms,

it seems—towers above the others. Looking far enough the
blossoming grasses take a purple tinge : yonder they are
riper and yellowish : still a bit further, a strip of woods,
and beyond, the mountains.   Out of the field, into the door-
yard of an old deserted house.   We pass that and enter a
beautiful woodsy road, nearly over-grown with grass and
low birches.   The trees on either side touch the wheels and
the horse's hoofs strike with a soft "pud—pud."

It is very still, the sunlight glints through the thick
foliage, falling with soft flecks of light on the dead leaves
and pine needles.   We find here that ghostly little flower—
the Indian pipe.   A little further and we strike the other
"old road" and as we descend the hill we get one of the
finest views of Amherst village, nestled into the greenery
of the noble elms.   A step or two more and we are beneath
the shade of these bending queens of the forest, back again
into the village.

THROUGH THE "DUGWAY" AND OVER CHESTNUT HILLS.

Starting from the village, we follow the Manchester road
as far as the bridge, at the foot of the hill, where the road
branches to right and left.   Keeping to the left and straight
ahead, we pass one or two points of interest i. e. the Isaac
Brooks Dodge homestead and the Jones place.   The former is a perfect store house of ancient relics, valuable on
account of age and the furore for such things, and as articles
of real historic worth.   The Jones house, among other

things quaintly savoring of "ye olden time," contains an amount of the Governor Winthrop furniture. After leaving this landmark behind us, the road leads through shaded ways to the foot of Mack's Hill, where there is one of the prettiest curves, serving as diplomatic introduction to a tedious climb up the steep hill. At the top is the old Mack house. The former occupants are prominent citizens of Lowell. From here there is a pleasant view of the village and over further rises the smoke from Nashua foundaries. A few steps further is the Secomb farm, from which wide awake men have gone to do their share of the world's work. Leaving the little district school to our left, we enter more wooded road, and commence a gentle ascent, and come shortly upon a level hill top. Over the crest of the hill and we enter what is called the "dugway," the wildest, prettiest drive in this vicinity, except that portion of the Mt. Vernon road, leading into Purgatory. It is a long slope, broken continually by little water sheds. Here stands the forest primeval, the young growth, tender vine and fern, all, in the fresh green of spring, the subdued verdure of summer time, the heavier coloring of autumn, mingled with the delicacy of gray mosses and green covered stones. Even in the barren winter season it is lovely, for the evergreen hemlocks and pines give life and color sufficient. On one side we look down into a narrow valley and the tops of large trees are on a level with the eye. A sharp turn to the right brings us on the valley road, along one side of which runs the brook, or, keeping straight on we may take another scramble over Chestnut Hills. The drive over the hill is long and hard but the air and view repay one for the effort. The view is wide and varied— village, city, lake, wood, field and mountain—even into the State of Maine the sight can reach — the air of bracing and exhilarating quality, is taken in long, deep breaths, and treasured in memory and lung, storehouses of mind and matter. The descent of the hill is necessarily so slowly made that the pleasure of its height is lost gradually, and the level home drive has its delight in meadow lily and field beauties, no less refreshing in a less ambitious way.

WALNUT HILL.

Walnut Hill in the north-east part of the town is worth a visit. The drive to it is pleasant, though in no way remarkable. But once up on the lower part of the hill, or on its summit one is surprised to find a view so wide and beautiful. There is a carriage road running through the fields belonging to Messrs. Whiting and Odell, where the cloud effects over the valley of the Souhegan and the mountains beyond are very fine. The near view is particularly pleasing. The proximity of the orchards and the corn fields and the partial height give one a sense of home protection and coziness, while the eye travels abroad and takes in the pleasure of the distance and wanders back again to the farm houses, and the laden apple trees. There is some-

thing truly human about an apple tree. It was so even in
our first knowledge of it in the Garden of Eden. Always
clustering in families, or standing with individual person-
ality near the home—with low wide spreading branches as
if for loving embrace. In what other fruit do we feel the
same sense of pleasure or disappointment so keenly as in
testing an apple? It is akin to our fancy toward new
friends. How——! but we digress. From the right of the
road one may leave his horse and make a hard climb up to
the top of the hill where he will see the pond with its dark
fringe of pines, lying at his feet, the Uncanoonucs over-
topping the hills farther to the north, Jo English, and following around to west and south, the whole range of distant
heights and the wide valley with its farms and villages. A
scene full of pastoral loveliness and peaceful comfort.

OVER PATCH HILL AND THE COUNTY BRIDGE.

Following the Milford road to the top of the hill we find
a road leading to the right, where a guide - post directs the
wayfarer toward Lyndeborough. That is our path. A
short journey on this road brings us to the top of Patch
hill. Pause here and look back upon the plain, and the
blue line of distant hills. This far distant, hazy line of
blue, is the nearest approach to a glimpse of the ocean we
have hereabouts. Elsewhere our height is too great, or
we are too near the hills to get this effect of a sea view. A
little farther on the view facing the Lyndeborough moun-

tains is pleasant.   Up on our right we see "Christian Hill."
From up there, this view over the mountain at sunset, re-
calls Pilgrim's Progress and the Delectable mountains.   It
always seems to us that the golden light over there is more
liquid than the sunset on any other point.   It reminds us
of those "streets of gold,"

A little new Jerusalem
Like to the one above.

But in a clear afternoon the color of rock and tree and field
seems more vivid—the distance enhanced by the dark belt
of pines seems greater—the scraps of wood and open road
seem more delightful up over Patch Hill, making it a pleas-
anter drive than over the higher one.

.After passing the berry farm of Benj. Wheeler, we enter
a pleasant bit of overhanging wood, whose green twilight is
refreshing in the summer time.   At the further entrance of
this strip, we cross a little brook : and right here stood the
first iron founadery erected in this vicinity. A portion of the
old dam is yet to be seen.   This low white house under
the great elms, was formerly the home of a family of Wool-
sons—grandparents of Miss Constance Fenimore Woolson.
It was one of this family, who planted the big elms on Amherst plain, though the credit of having it done belongs to
Dr. Spaulding.   At the second cross of the roads is a building, now used as a mill, a portion of which was formerly
the old village school house.

.At the next intersection of the roads we turn sharply to the
left and soon turn again to the right.   We pass the home-

stead and family burial ground of the Hutchinson family
of musical celebrity. The next turn is to the left and we
soon arrive at the County Bridge. Formerly the river was
forded at this point. Considering how rocky its bed is, the
bridge must have been an accession greatly rejoiced at by
the nervous ones. Crossing the railroad track, we find ourselves out on a broad, level road, shaded the greater part of
its length by beautiful elms, which gives it its name—
Elm street. This street leads directly into Milford village
from the west. In Milford village we leave the common
on our right, and are once again on the familiar road to
Amherst.

Other drives there are as beautiful as these. Some that
others count more beautiful—but these are the first that
come to mind and the most frequently travelled—that drive
to Mont Vernon, coming into Mont Vernon from the north
and climbing Prospect Hill, from which point there is the
most extensive view to be procured ; again, those drives
to the Uncanoonuc—to the Pulpit—to Purgatory—to New
Boston—all beautiful and full of the charm of variety. We
only mention those near home.

MONT VERNON.

"The Bethlehem of Southern New Hampshire."

[From an article in the FARMERS' CABINET, Aug. 22, 1889.]

MONT VERNON, for nearly forty years past a famous summer resort, lies a little southward from the territorial centre of Hillsborough county, being third in the tier of towns northward from the Massachusetts line. It is 50 miles from Boston, 28 from Concord and 15 from Manchester. The nearest railroad station is Milford, 4 1-2 miles, with which it is connected by a stage line. It is emphatically an upland town, the larger part being a lofty ridge between the valleys of the south branch of the Piscataquog river on the north and that of the Souhegan on the south. The soil is rocky, but deep and fertile, repaying careful cultivation. It is well adapted to the apple, several thousand barrels being the annual product of its orchards, and the winter apples grown here have long been noted as unexcelled for their keeping qualities. The annual crop of blueberries gathered from its pastures is many hundred bushels.

The highest elevation in Mont Vernon is Roby Hill, in the northeast part of the town near Jo's Pond, other conspicuous prominences are McCollom's Hill, on the norther-

ly line of the town, Beach Hill, and near the village, easterly and southeasterly, are Campbell's Hill and Prospect
Hill. From the summit of the latter, which is a broad and
pleasant plateau, at an altitude of 100 feet above the village,
is obtained a prospect most varied and magnificent. An expanse of country forty miles in every direction, is seen with
the naked eye. Hundreds of visitors are attracted thither
every year to admire and enjoy the landscape which this
noble hill presents to view. Cottages are in process of
erection on the hill, and doubtless in the near future its
whole area will be covered with elegant structures for summer occupancy.

Mont Vernon is on an eminence nearly 800 feet above
mean tide water, with its church, academy and a number
of its elegant residences resting on the brow of the hill
looking southward upon a landscape stretching 40 miles
away in beauty and grandeur. It has 42 dwellings built
mainly upon one street. Here is the Bellevue House, a fine
four story sructure, used as the village hotel, and accomo-
dating 40 summer guests. Four other large and handsome
boarding houses will convene 130 guests. These are "Conant Hall," "Prospect House," "Hillsborough House," and
the "Deanery." Aside from these are eight or ten commodious boarding houses, which with those already noted, furnish spacious and elegant accommodations for 300 guests,
which is the usual number from the middle of July to Sept.

The village, though small, is by common consent pronounced one of the most beautiful in New Hampshire, the
elements of which are its well-kept, shady streets, and the
are of neatness and thrift, not one of its dwellings being
other than in a creditable condition and the grandly beautiful prospect it commands in all directions. It is often
remarked that Mont Vernon is a good place to visit the

second season. The air is remarkably dry and bracing. The best physicians affirm its purity and health-giving properties are not to be excelled by any place in New Hampshire, which, with the liberal provision for the enjoyment and comfort of guests, induces the return of many year after year, and it has become known to thousands as a most delightful resort for seekers of health and rest.

It was in 1855 that F. O. Kittredge, then an active and enterprising citizen and still a summer resident, perceiving the advantages of the town as a summer resort purchased the old Ray tavern in the centre of the village, where is now the beautiful park, remodelled and enlarged it and fitting and furnishing it in an elegant and tasteful manner, opened it for summer company. For 13 years it was thronged in the hot season. In 1868 the proprietor enlarged and extended it to three times its former size, giving it a height of four stories and a length of one hundred and forty-five feet surmounted by a cupola in the centre. As completed it was a stately and beautiful structure ; one of the largest and best appointed public houses in New Hampshire. April 20, 1872, it was burned to the ground by a fire which commenced in the attic. Not being rebuilt its loss has been a severe blow to the prosperity and growth of the village.

About two miles from the village, near the westerly line, is "Purgatory Falls," a remarkable natural curiosity much frequented by excursionists from far and near.

Fifty years since the village was a centre of considerable trade. Located on a leading thoroughfare from Boston to Vermont the tide of travel and transportation gave it life and stir and supported three stores and three taverns. Railway service has made the stage coach and six-horse merchandise wagon a tradition. In 1837 the building which stood 56 years on the easterly side of the common fronting southward was removed westerly and entirely remodelled, so as to remove all semblance of the old structure, though the frame is the old church of 1781.

The Post office here was established in 1813. Prior to that time letters for the inhabitants were distributed from Amherst. How is the anomally explained that the legal name of the office is Mount Vernon, and that of the town Mont Vernon, is a question often asked. It occurs in the fact that in 1869, Mr. Kittredge owned and occupied the grand summer house which was "The Mount Vernon House." It was desirable to him that the post-office, town and hotel should correspond in name, consequently a petition to Washington brought a new name for the post-office. The town has never chosen to amend the unique and melodious name it has borne well nigh a century.

The salubrity of the breezes which fan Mont Vernon is attested to by the fact which patient research has ascertained, that considerably over 200 persons, who were residents of the town in 1820, or who have since lived here for the term of 25 years have reached the age of 80 years.

The church has existed here 109 years, 105 of which it has had a settled ministry. Mr. John Bruce, from Marlborough, Mass., commenced preaching here in the summer of 1784, was ordained the following year, and continued his labors until his sudden death in 1809. The present pastor, Rev. John Thorpe, is the 14th in succession from Mr. Bruce. The longest pastorate that has closed was the first of 25 years, and the shortest was the last of two years.

In former years this town was noted more than now for its distinctive religious character. "Mount Zion" it has been irreverently called. The views of the controling majority in the early history of the Parish are shown by the

record : "March 25th. 1792.   Voted that the bass viol be
not carried into the meeting house to be used in time of
exercise."

An act incorporating the town of Mont Vernon was con-
sumated by the signature of Gov. T. Gilman, Dec. 15,
1803.   The name of the town, (a compound word signify-
ing a mountain of verdure) was suggested by the verdure
of the farms which cluster about the eminence upon which
the village is located.

A conspicuous feature in Mont Vernon is its Academy,
known as McCollom Institute.   Nearly every autumn from
1830 to 1850, there had been kept in the village a select
school usually taught by a fresh college graduate.

Enterprising citizens appreciating the many elements
which marked the noble eminence as a desirable locality for
public education, associated together and in June of the
latter year obtained an act of incorporation for a projected
school, to be called Appleton Academy.   Eight citizens of
the town were trustees, and Dr. S. G. Dearborn, now of
Nashua, was Secretary.   The first term was taught in the
fall of 1850, in the hall now known as the church vestry.
As an evidence of the high hopes cherished by its founders
for its success, is the fact they procured for its first term as
teachers, two recent graduates from a New England college,
one of whom is now a most respectable New Hampshire
lawyer and his assistant is a most eminent professor in New
York city.   In 1853 the fine building it now occupies was
erected, and in one year was free from debt.   In 1871, Geo.
W. McCollom of New York, in early life a resident of Mont
Vernon, offered the institution $10,000 in addition to its
permanent fund upon the acceptance of certain conditions,
which being acceded to it became "McCollom Institute."
The institution has had an existence of 39 years, during

which 13 gentlemen have held the office of Principal and a large corps of assistant teachers, 1,600 persons have been enrolled as students. The attendance has varied from 25 to 125. Among its notable preceptors has been Hon. Geo. Stevens of Lowell, deceased; Rev. Augustus Berry of Pelham; Principal C. F. P. Bancroft of Andover; Prof. W. H. Ray of Chicago, deceased, and Prof. C. S. Campbell of Derry. Its invested cash fund exceeding $13,000 is respectable, yet more would be acceptable. It has a most valuable and extensive apparatus for the illustration of physical science and a library of 4200 volumes. Among those who have enjoyed its advantages are many who in the learned professions are distinguished and in public service honored and hundreds more as really useful, often conspicuous, who are ready to testify their attachment and gratitude for the strength and help this institution has given them for the conflict of life.

PERSONAL.

Most conspicuous among the citizens of Mont Vernon, was Dr. Daniel Adams. He came here from Massachusetts in 1813, at the age of 40, thoroughly educated, and was engaged in the preparation of his various publications and in his profession here, until he removed to Keene, in 1846. His various arithmetics were in very extensive use for many years. During his 33 years residence in Mont Vernon he wielded a controlling influence in behalf of temperance, education and morality. While here he represented the district two years, 1839 and 1840, in the New Hampshire Senate.

Aaron F. Sawyer was a very respectable lawyer here for 25 years from 1807, to 1832, when he removed to Nashua. He died there in 1846. He represented Mont Vernon from 1827-9, three years, and was the only lawyer who practised here for any length of time.

Among those who left a record honoring the place of their birth may be mentioned the late Dr. William Trevitt of Columbus, Ohio. Born in Mont Vernon in 1809. He prepared for his profession in New England and emigrated to Ohio at 21, was returned to the General Assembly of Ohio at 26, serving three terms, was some five years physician to the Ohio Penitentiary; during the entire Mexican war was a distinguished surgeon of the army, afterwards for four years Secretary of State of Ohio, U. S. Consul to Valparaiso, So. Chili, and U. S. Minister to Peru. He died in 1881, esteemed by all parties, and after a very active and eventful life.

George Wilkins Kendall, born in Mont Vernon in 1809 and dying in Texas in 1867. He was a "poet, journalist and farmer," and eminent in all.

Oliver Carleton, Esq., of Salem, Mass., born at Mont Vernon, in 1801, died in 1882. Educated at Dartmouth, where he was a tutor, was 25 years Master of the Salem Latin School and afterwards of a celebrated private school. As a chemical scholar and tutor he was hardly equalled in New England.

Hon. Samuel L. Sawyer of Independence, Mo., oldest son of Aaron F., was educated at Dartmouth, studied law with his father, went west, and many years since located in Missouri, where he has been a judge of the Supreme Court and Representative in Congress. His younger brother, Hon. Aaron W. Sawyer of Nashua, was born in 1818 and died in 1881; was frequently a member of the Legislature, was Mayor of Nashua and a Judge of the Supreme Judicial Court. He attained a high reputation as a lawyer and jurist. Late in life he became interested in religion and preached the Gospel with zealous ability.

Hon. George A. Marden of Lowell, Mass., over twenty years editor of the Lowell COURIER, and widely known in journalism and politics, was 9 years clerk of the Massachusetts House of Representatives, two years its Speaker, one year a Senator and now holds the position of Treasurer and Receiver General of Massachusetts.

Hon. George A. Bruce of Somerville, Mass., is a Boston lawyer of assured reputation and lucrative practice both as counsellor and advocate. He was three years Mayor of Somerville, two years in the Massachusetts Senate and one year its president, and did he seek them could easily attain higher honors.

But space forbids mention of the hosts of other sons and daughters of the little town who have gone forth to careers of active usefulness and now are shedding by life and character lustre upon the place of their birth and early training.

-Conant ✳ Hall-

Is located in the pleasant village of Mont Vernon, N. H., fifty miles from Boston, on an elevation a thousand feet above the level of the sea, commanding an extended and varied prospect. Its easy communication with Boston, its pleasant walks and drives, and healthy location, render it one of the most desirable places in New England in which to spend the summer months.

CONANT HALL, MONT VERNON.   [Open June to Nov.]

Ample grounds with shade trees around house.   Good stable and laundry.   Visitors take the cars at the Boston & Lowell depot for Milford, N. H. thence by stage to Mont Vernon, four miles from the station.   Four daily train. to and from Boston.

If desired, shall be happy to furnish reference from among our numerous patrons in Boston and vicinity.

For further information call on Bragg, Conant & Co., 16 Washington St., A. Conant & Co., 73 Union St., Boston.

Bellevue House.

MONT VERNON, N. H.

Accomodates from 50 to 60, with large airy rooms.

GOOD TABLE BOARD.

Pure Air, Extended Views,
Good Roads, Shady Drives,
Hunting and Fishing.

Our principal means of advertising is through our patrons. and references of this kind are cheerfully furnished.

TERMS: Regular board $1.00 per day : transient rates. $2.00 per day.

W. P. WOODS,   -   Proprietor.

Prospect Cottage

NEW BOSTON, N. H.

Open for Boarders from June 15th to Oct. 1st.

Very pleasantly situated on high ground, commanding a lovely view ; ten minutes walk from post-office, stores and Whipple Free Library, to which all visitors have access. Good house, piazzas, bath room, shade trees, hammocks, croquet, lawn-tennis, etc. ; piano and organ : sitting and dining room apart from family. Near Uncanoonuc Mountains, Devil's Pulpit, Purgatory, etc. All country luxuries. Terms reasonable. For circulars address,

Mrs. S. D. Atwood, New Boston,

Hillsboro' County, New Hampshire.

"The Greenwood."

NEW BOSTON N. H.

One of the most desirable places for summer boarding. Charmingly located in New Boston, upper village, on high ground, within few minutes walk of post office, stores, churches, Whipple Free Library, etc. Scenery unsurpassed, abundance of shade trees, piazzas, lawn-tennis and croquet grounds. Pleasant walks and drives in all directions.

Reached by way of Manchester to Parker's Station, where coach connects twice a day with trains from Boston.

Mrs. George Greenwood.

New Boston, N. H.

❖Hotel Ponemah.❖

D. S. PLUMMER, Proprietor.

The house is handsomely furnished, with latest modern improvements. Its sanitarian is perfect. To those who would add to the tonic of mountain air and the freedom of country living the comforts and luxuries of a first-class hotel, the Ponemah offers unrivalled inducements for summer residence. A large boarding and livery stable is connected with the hotel. The grounds include about forty acres of superb groves of oak, pine, maple and chestnut trees, and contain the celebrated Ponemah and Milford Springs.

Ponemah water bottled at the spring is unequalled as a pure, healthful, sparkling table water, and is furnished to guests free.

Plans of hotel may be seen and rooms secured on application to Barnes & Duncklee, proprietors of Hotels Brunswick and Victoria, Boston, or to C. A. Gleason, Hotel Victoria.

Prices according to location of room. Special rates by the season or week.

Address after June 1st, D. S. PLUMMER, Proprietor, Amherst Station, N. H.

www.ingramcontent.com/pod-product-compliance
Lightning Source LLC
Chambersburg PA
CBHW030018030726
47499CB00008B/3047